PROFESSOR WHISKERTON PRESENTS

STEAMPUNK ABC

written and illustrated by **LISA FALKENSTERN**

two lions

two lions

Amazon Publishing
Attn: Amazon Children's Publishing
P.O. Box 400818
Las Vegas, NV 89140
www.amazon.com/amazonchildrenspublishing

Library of Congress Cataloging-in-Publication Data is available upon request.

ISBN-13: 9781477847220 (hardcover)
ISBN-10: 1477847227 (hardcover)
ISBN-13: 9781477897225 (eBook)
ISBN-10: 1477897224 (eBook)

Book design by Katrina Damkoehler
Editor: Margery Cuyler

Printed in China (R)
First edition
10 9 8 7 6 5 4 3 2 1

To Ken,
you are everything to me

A is for anvil.

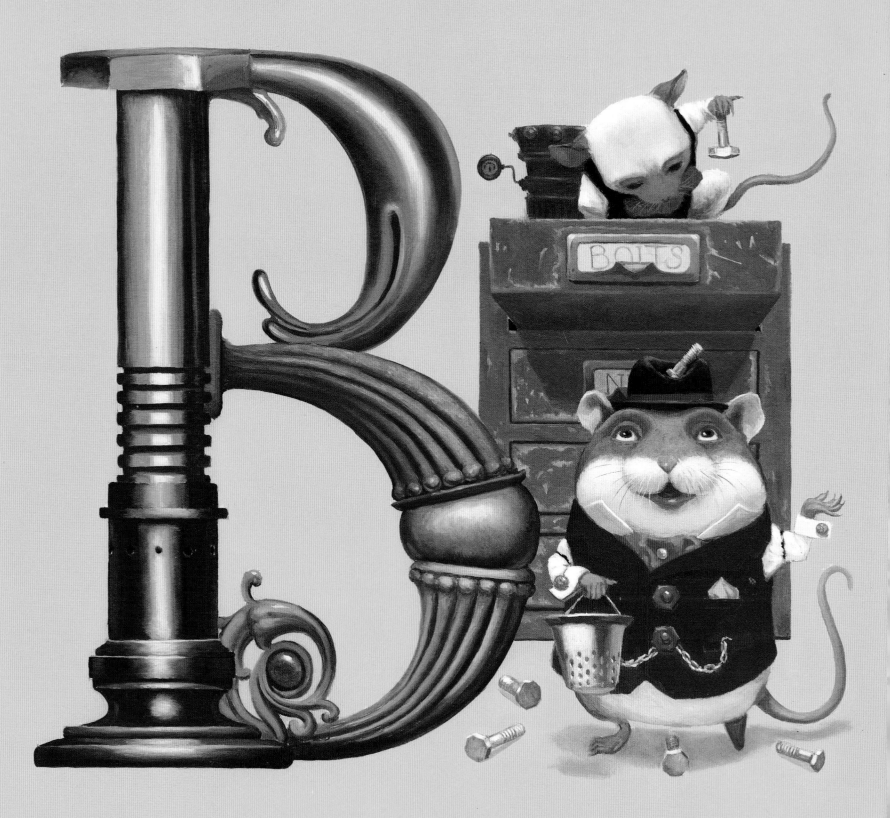

B is for bolt.

C is for crank.

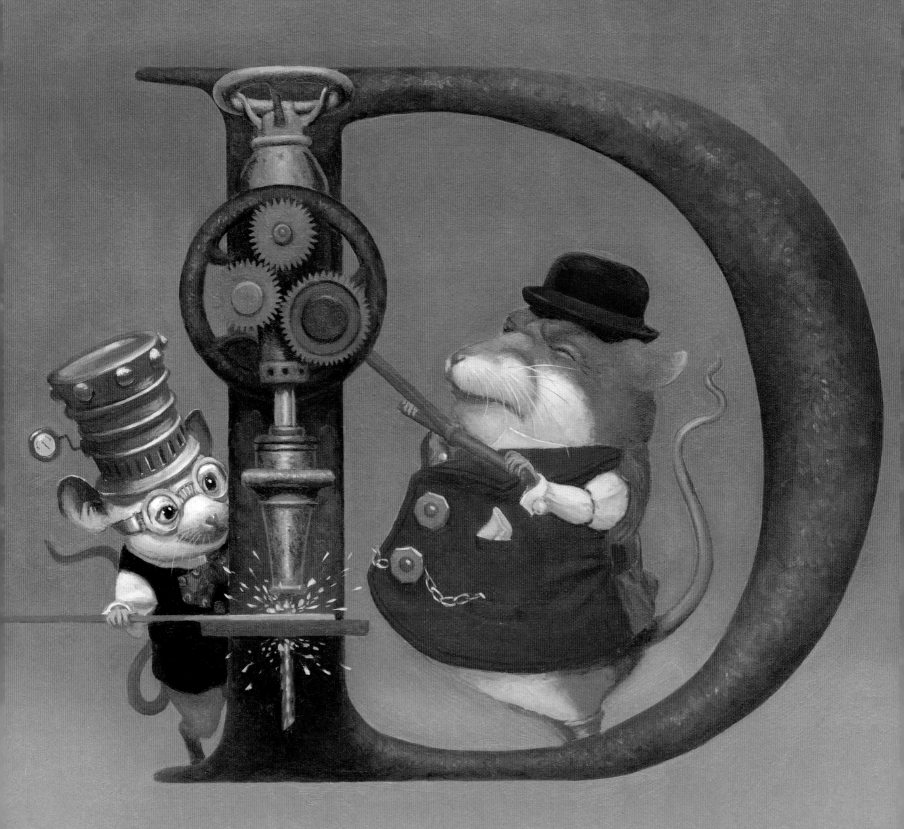

D is for drill.

E is for elevator.

F is for faucet.

G is for gear.

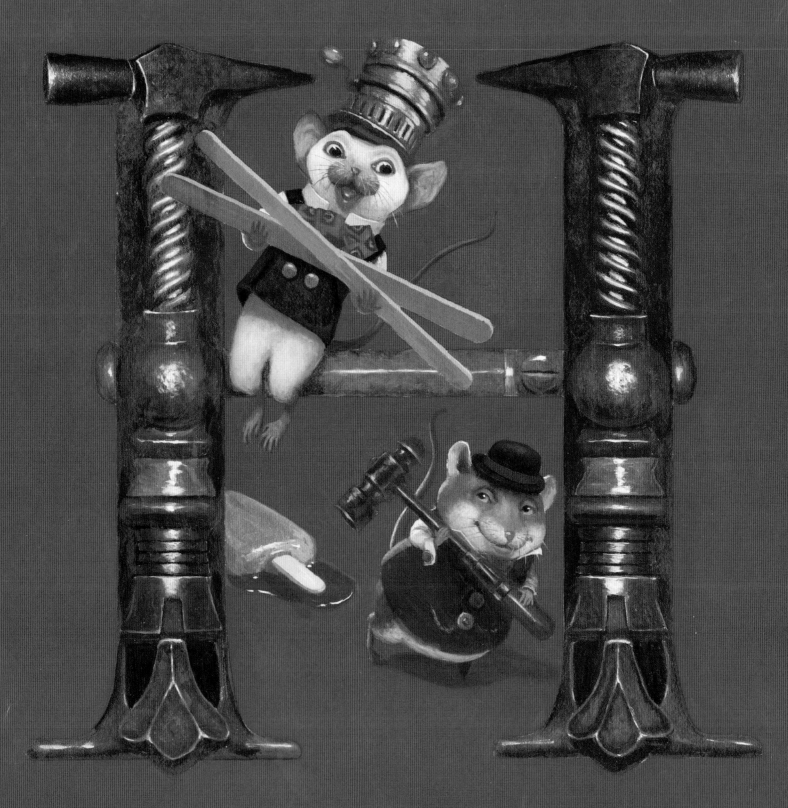

H is for hammer.

I is for iron.

J is for joint.

K is for kettle.

L is for level.

M is for monkey wrench.

N is for nail.

O is for oil.

P is for periscope.

Q is for quartz.

R is for rivet.

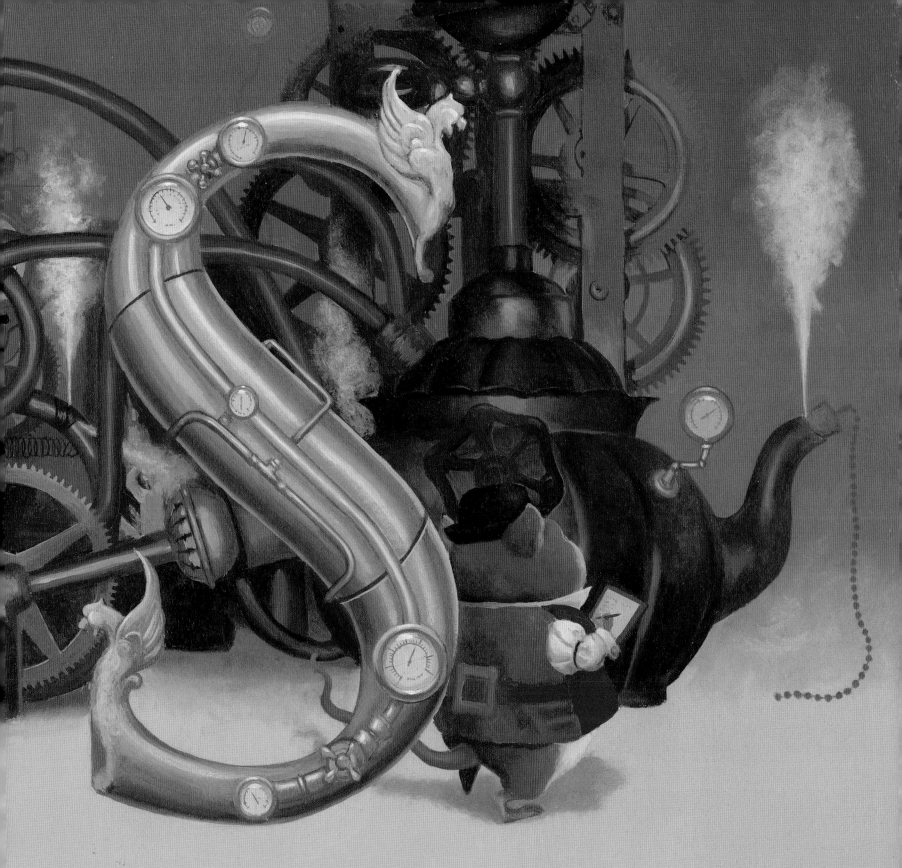

S is for steam.

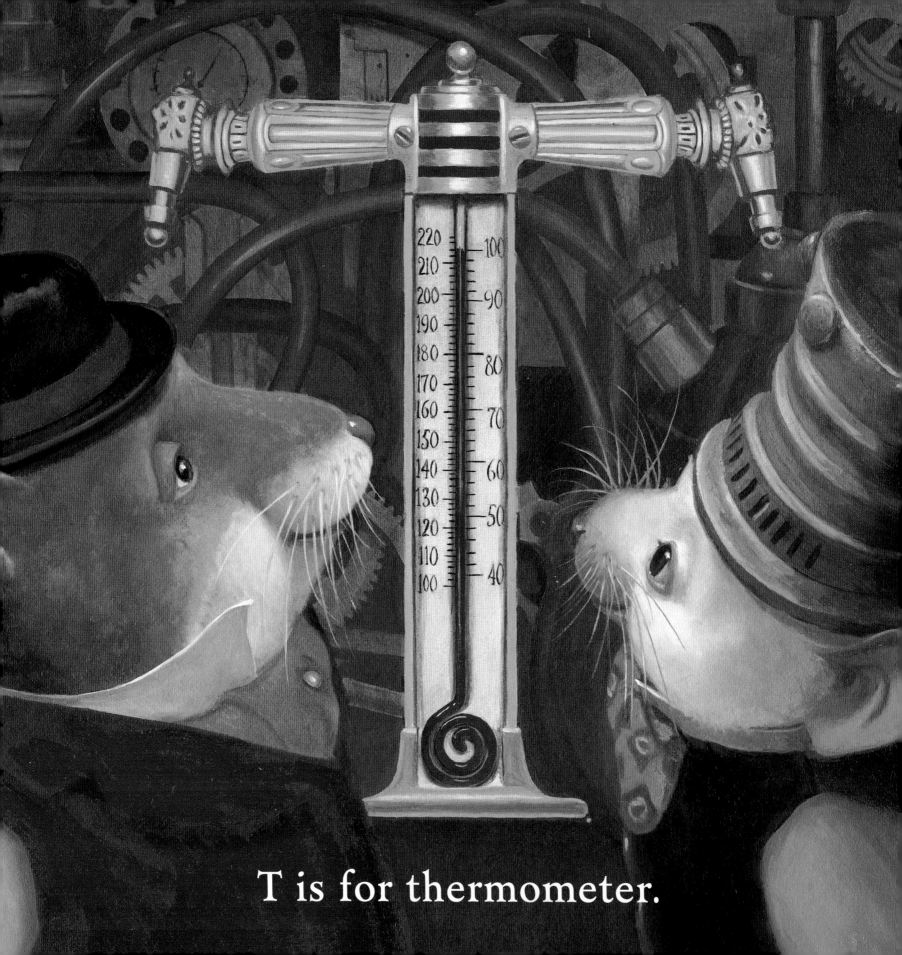

T is for thermometer.

U is for uniform.

V is for valve.

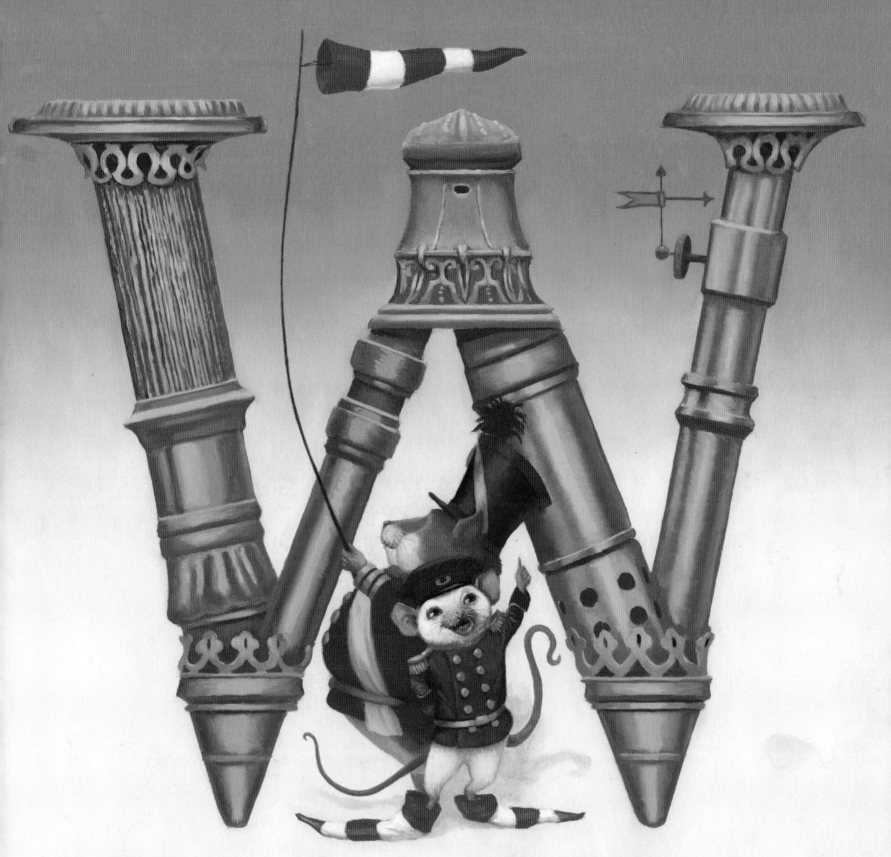

W is for windsock.

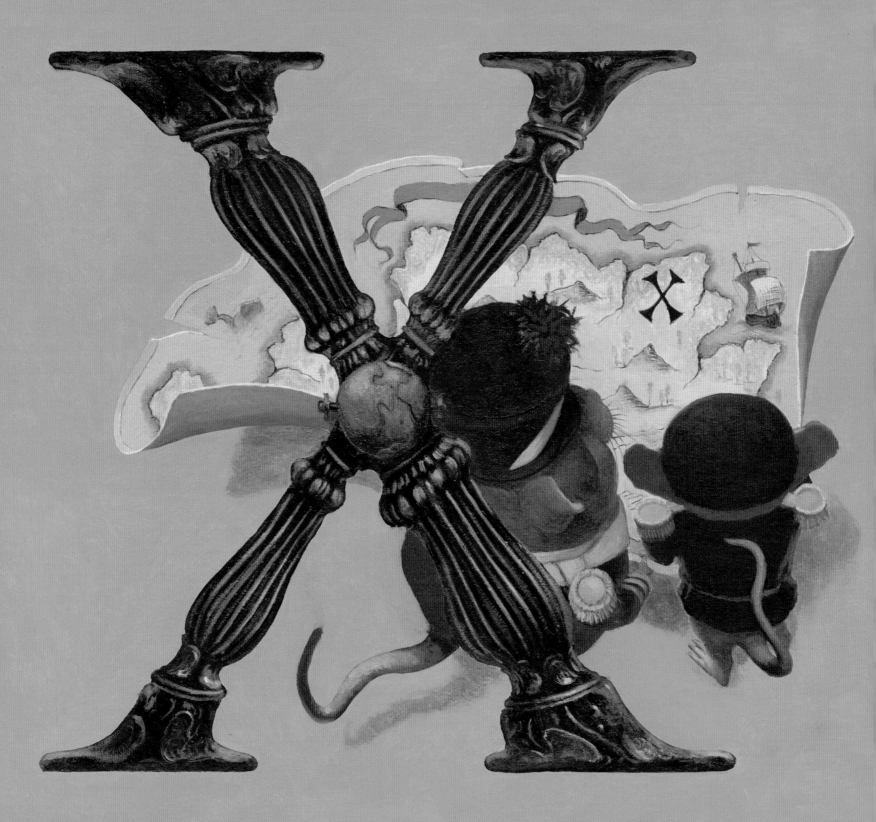

X is for X marks the spot.

Y is for yellow.

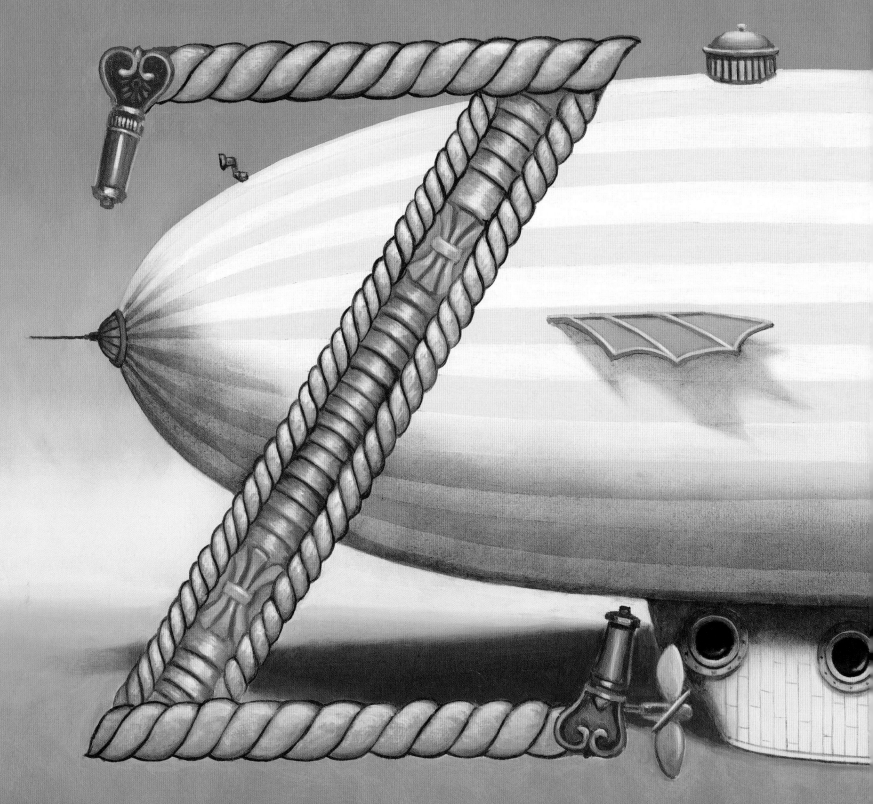

Z is for zeppelin.